GRIMM

The Musicians of Bremen

Illustrated by Svend Otto S.

Translated by Anne Rogers

Larousse & Co., Inc.

There was once an old donkey who had carried sacks
for the miller for many a long year. But now he was
getting too weak-kneed to work, and he guessed that
his master would soon want to get rid of him. So
one day he ran away and trotted off towards
Bremen to find a job as a musician. For he liked the
sound of his own voice, and even dreamed of
accompanying himself on the lute.

He hadn't gone far when he came to an old dog lying by the path, panting as if he had been running for hours.

"What's the matter?" asked the donkey.

"I'm worn out," said the dog. "I'm too old for hunting, so my master said he would get rid of me. I've run away, but what's the use? How can I keep going?"

"Cheer up," said the donkey. "I'm going to Bremen to find a job as a musician. Why don't you come too as my drummer?"

"But I haven't got a drum," said the dog sadly.

"We can soon buy one in Bremen," said the donkey.

The dog thought that a brilliant idea. He had got his breath back by now, and eagerly set off with the donkey. They hadn't gone far when they came to an old cat sitting shivering by the path.

"What's the matter?" asked the donkey.

"Nobody wants me," sighed the cat. "I'm too old to chase mice, and my teeth are beginning to fall out. My mistress said she would get rid of me, so I ran away to save her the trouble. But it hasn't done me much good so far. Where shall I go now?"

"Cheer up," said the donkey. "Come along with us to Bremen. You can sing soprano, can't you? Well then, we'll make our fortune together."

The cat thought that a brilliant idea. The three trotted along till they came to a farm. On the gate a cock was crowing desperately, as if his life depended on it.

"You certainly can sing," said the donkey.
"What's it all about?"

"The farmer's wife has asked visitors to dinner tomorrow, and I heard her say she'll make me into chicken soup. So I'm making as much noise as I can; it's my last chance."

"Cheer up," said the donkey. "Come along with us to Bremen. We can do with an extra voice. You can be our tenor – that's a better idea than being made into soup, isn't it?"

The cock thought it was a brilliant idea, and the four friends went on their way together.

Soon they came to a forest, and as it was getting
dark, they began to look for a place to sleep. The
donkey and the dog lay down under a tree, the cat
curled up on a bough and the cock fluttered up to
one of the highest branches. From this high perch
he could see a light shining through a window. So
he told his friends there must be a house a little
further on.

The dog agreed. With luck he might find a bone
or two; perhaps there would even be some meat left

on one of them. They all followed their noses and
made straight for the lighted window.

They crept up to the house, but the donkey was
the only one tall enough to see inside.

"What can you see?" asked the cock.

"Haw, haw, what can I see?" said the donkey. "A table with plenty to eat and drink—just what we want—and six robbers tucking in."

"Then there won't be anything left for us," said the cock.

"Oh yes, there will," said the donkey, "if we use our wits."

So they all tried hard to think of a way to turn the robbers out of the house and settle there themselves. At last they had a brilliant idea—they would sing for their supper. The donkey stood with his forefeet on the window-sill, the dog jumped on to his back, the cat climbed on top of the dog and the cock flew on to the cat's head.

When they were all ready, the donkey said: "SING!" They all sang fortissimo and frightened the robbers so much that they rushed off into the forest, sure that terrifying monsters were after them.

The four musicians felt that their plan had worked splendidly. They lost no time in getting to the table, finding their favourite food and gobbling as much as they could eat.

They soon felt very full and floppy, and looked round for somewhere to sleep. They put out the light, and the donkey lay down on some straw in the yard, the dog crouched in a corner behind the back door and the cat curled up on

the warm hearth. The cock flew up and perched on a high rafter. And they all fell fast asleep.

At one o'clock, at dead of night, the robbers came out from their hiding places and saw that the house was quite dark.

"It's all right, we can go back now," whispered their leader. "We shouldn't have been scared off so easily." But he did not feel as brave as he sounded, so he sent one of the others back to make sure that the house was empty.

He crept cautiously back and couldn't hear a
sound, so he went into the kitchen to light a candle.
He could see the cat's eyes glimmering in the hearth
and mistook them for live coals. Bending down, he
tried to light a match by them. The cat didn't find
this at all funny. She flew in his face, spitting and
scratching.

The robber was terrified. He groped his way

to the back door, but before he reached it the
dog jumped up and bit his leg. As he ran across
the yard, the donkey gave him a sharp kick and
the cock crowed with a piercing shriek from the
rafter: "*Cockadoodle doo! Cockadoodle doo!*"

Rushing back to the others, the robber told
them how he had been treated: "There's a

wicked witch in the house—she spat at me and
scratched my face with her long nails. And
there's an armed man hiding behind the door—as
I came out he stabbed me in the leg. In the yard
there's a great hairy monster, who beat me with his
club, and—worst of all—on the roof there's an old
judge; when he saw me he yelled: '*Catch that crook!*
Catch that crook!'"

By now the robbers were all quite sure that the
house was no place for them, and they were soon
miles away. But the four musicians settled in very

comfortably. They were in no hurry to go on to Bremen. They all agreed that it would be silly to leave a good home that suited them so well, and I expect they are still there.